GOBLIN
in the city

For Millie. S.M.K.

For Luke, Beth and Jacob. V.K.

Random House Australia Pty Ltd
20 Alfred Street, Milsons Point, NSW 2061
http://www.randomhouse.com.au

Sydney   New York   Toronto
London   Auckland   Johannesburg

First published by Random House Australia 2004
Text copyright © Victor Kelleher 2004
Illustrations copyright © Stephen Michael King 2004

National Library of Australia
Cataloguing-in-Publication Entry

       Kelleher, Victor, 1939- .
       Goblin in the city.

       Children aged 6 years and over.
       ISBN 1 74051 981 7.

       1. Goblins - Juvenile fiction. 2. City and town life -
       Juvenile fiction. I. King, Stephen Michael. II. Title.

    A823.3

Cover design by Jobi Murphy and Stephen Michael King
Internal design by Jobi Murphy
Typeset by Jobi Murphy in Lemonade
Printed and bound by Griffin Press, Netley, South Australia

10 9 8 7 6 5 4 3 2 1

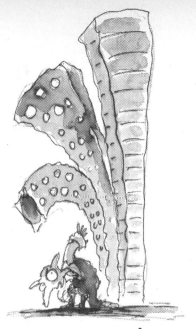

GOBLIN
in the city

**Victor Kelleher and
Stephen Michael King**

RANDOM HOUSE AUSTRALIA

CHAPTER ONE

Irish goblins are a miserable lot.
Yet, for once, Gibblewort the goblin
felt content. He lay curled up in a
postbag, on board a jet plane.

Why did that make him happy?
Because he thought he was leaving
Australia. He'd been sent here by his
goblin mates, as a punishment for
being too wicked. Now, at last,
he was on his way home to Ireland.
He could hardly wait to get revenge
on the other goblins.

'I'll soon be makin' their lives a
misery,' he chuckled.

What he didn't know was that the
address on his postbag was wet
and smudged. No one could read it.
So instead of flying off to Ireland,
he was heading for the lost
property office in Sydney.

He gave a wicked laugh when the
plane touched down. He thought
he'd arrived home.

'Goblins beware,' he chuckled,
sharpening his pointy nails.

He wasn't quite so pleased when
someone threw his postbag off
the plane.

"Ouch!"

he said, as he landed on
the tarmac.

Someone else tossed the bag onto
a trolley filled with spiky parcels.

"Yoiks!" he yelled.

Next, he was shoved into
a van. Heavy parcels were
heaped on top of him.

"H-e-l-p!"

he squeaked.

This was no way to treat a goblin.
It put him in a horrible temper.

'Blither and blather!' he roared,
and kicked a hole in the postbag.
A second kick sent parcels flying.
A third kick burst open the back
doors of the van.

But wait a minute! The sky was clear.

The sun was shining. It was hot!

This couldn't be Ireland. Surely!

Where were the grey clouds?

Where was the squelchy rain?

Where were the icy breezes?

Gibblewort leant out of the van
for a better look. Then he leant a
little further... lost his balance ...
and fell splat onto the road.

He sat up and looked around. He
had landed in the middle of a noisy,
smelly, crowded, busy city.

CHAPTER
TWO

Gibblewort had always lived in the country. He had never seen traffic like this. There were buses to his right. Giant semis to his left. Cars and vans everywhere.

Horns hooted; drivers shouted; exhaust fumes made him sneeze.

'Oh, my!' he moaned. 'Where have they hidden peaceful old Ireland?'

But he was in luck. A passing cyclist scooped him up and tossed him onto the pavement.

'Goblins be praised!' he thought...
until he looked up at the buildings.
They were nearly touching the
clouds! They seemed
about to topple
onto his bald
head.

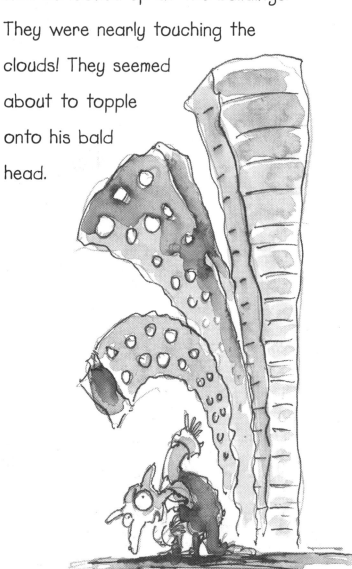

With a yelp, he dived through the nearest doorway, straight into a bookshop.

Gibblewort's warty nose turned pale. So did his hairy ears. After bathtubs, books were the things he hated most. And here were thousands of them! Enough bedtime reading to put him to sleep forever!

He was about to tiptoe
out when he noticed a
counter that sold ink.
Now, Gibblewort loved blue-
coloured ink. He managed to drink
three bottles before a shop
assistant grabbed him.

She tried to drag him off to the
manager, but he poked out his
bright blue tongue, and she fell
down in a faint.

Gibblewort escaped
by scuttling into
the supermarket
next door.

This was more
like it! On the
nearest shelf
he could see his
favourite lollies.

Moth balls! He crunched up a whole
heap, and followed them with his
second favourite: soap powder!

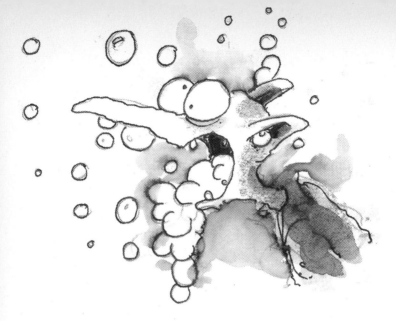

Halfway through a big packet, he began foaming at the mouth. And the nose! And the ears! What with his blue tongue and all that foam, people thought he was a monster.

Customers screamed. More shop assistants fainted. Mums and dads rushed out through the exits, leaving their shopping behind.

Gibblewort was having a wonderful time. He was just thinking up more nasty tricks when he spotted a security guard striding towards him.

'Time to go, boyo,' muttered Gibblewort, and joined the rush for the exit.

'Hey! You haven't paid!' the checkout girl yelled, and also gave chase.

Gibblewort hadn't run so fast in a long time. Along the pavement he sped, knocking old ladies over as he went. Across the road he hopped, dodging the traffic. Down a lane he hurried.

He could hardly believe what lay before him. Not more buildings. Not more shops. Here was something far better. A big green space, full of trees and grass, with a children's playground in one corner.

Gibblewort gave an evil grin. This was his kind of place. He would scare everyone else away and have it all to himself.

Or so he thought.

CHAPTER
THREE

Gibblewort pulled his ugliest face
as he strode into the park. He
bulged out his eyes. He crinkled
up his nose. He waggled his ears.
He bared his brown fangs and
let spit dribble off the ends.

Grown-ups screamed and ran off.
But not the kids.

'Wow, a creature from outer
space!' they cried.

They grabbed his ears. They
tweaked his nose. They tugged his
greasy hair. Some copied his bulgy-
eyed look and made spit trickle
down their chins.

Gibblewort tried to get away by
climbing up the slide. He changed
his mind when he reached the top,
but it was too late. The kids
shoved him off.

Down the slide he whooshed,
shrieking all the way.

'A-A-A-A-A-Agh!'

At the bottom, he took off and
sailed through the air.

'He really is from outer space!' the
kids said. 'Look at him fly!'

He landed with an awful bump on
the roundabout.

'Let's make him fly again!' the kids
said, and pushed the
roundabout faster.

'Ooh!' Gibblewort whimpered.

He was hanging on only by his
hands. Then his nails. Then by
nothing at all.

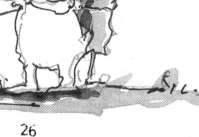

He landed on a swing.

'Blast-off time!' the kids said, and
pushed him higher.

He was clinging on only
by his hands. Then his
nails. Then by
nothing at all.

How blue the sky looked as he sailed up into it. How green the ground looked as he rushed down to meet it.

The bump made his fangs rattle.

'Twinkle, twinkle...' he muttered in a dazed voice.

He had landed inside the climbing
frame. There were strong bars all
around him. He thought he was in
prison. Kids crowded against the
bars, trying to feed him stuff.
Horrible stuff. Food that goblins
can't bear.
Like ice cream,
and chips,
and chocolate.

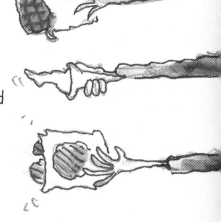

Oh, what he would
have given for a
nice bag
of moth balls.
Or better still,
a juicy worm.

CHAPTER FOUR

Gibblewort had to get away from these kids. They were worse than goblins! So he scrambled up the bars and jumped out of the climbing frame.

It wasn't his day. He landed on a skateboard.

Whoosh, went the skateboard, straight down the path.

'Is there no solid ground around here?' he whimpered.

'Yay, look at him go!' the kids said, and raced after him.

Still on the skateboard, Gibblewort zoomed across the park and through the heavy traffic.

'Hoot-hoot! Honk-honk!'

He was headed for a tall building.

It had a weird sort of entrance.

A revolving door!

Round and round and round he went. He was really dizzy when he popped out on the other side.

'Won't some kindly soul hold the world still?' he pleaded, and staggered into an open lift.

An extra-fast lift!

The doors slid closed.
The lift whooshed to the top of the building.

Gibblewort felt quite ill by the time it stopped. And much worse when he crawled across the roof and looked down.

'What have they done with the ground?' he wondered in a scared voice.

He soon found out, because he lost his balance and tipped over the edge.

Down, down, down he fell.

'Maybe it's a bird I'm turnin' into,' he said, and fluttered his arms.

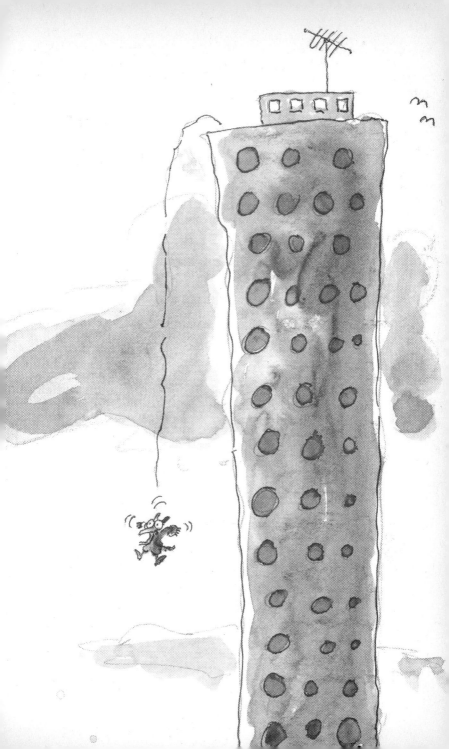

It didn't help. He landed with a
crunch, head-first. That didn't hurt
Gibblewort much, but his rock-hard
head made a big crack in the
pavement.

'Ooh!' he said, rubbing his bald
spot.

When he stood up, a policeman was staring at him. So were the security guard, and the kids from the park.

The policeman pointed to the cracked pavement.

'I'm arresting you for damage to public property,' he said in a stern voice.

At that moment, another door
slid open. Right next to them.
Gibblewort leapt through.

And then… and then… everything
started to move. The whole city
this time! Faster and faster it went.

'Stop the world!' Gibblewort
groaned. 'I want to get off!'

CHAPTER FIVE

Gibblewort didn't realise he'd boarded a bus.

'Ting,' went the bell.

Straight away he felt better.
He watched a passenger press
a little red button.

'Ting,' went the bell again, and his blubbery lips stretched into a grin.

Bells are like heavenly music to goblins. They can't get enough of them. Gibblewort reached up and pushed the button over and over.

'Ting, ting, ting, ting, ting, ting, ting, ting, ting, ting, ting.'

'Aah, I'm in heaven after all,' he sighed.

But not for long. The bus
screeched to a stop.

'I'm fed up with you naughty kids,'
the driver said. 'And get rid of
that silly mask,' he added, as he
kicked Gibblewort off the bus.

Gibblewort landed in the back
of a ute. He shared it with a
fierce dog. It had fangs longer
than any goblin's, and a nasty
look in its eyes.

'G-r-r-r-r!' went the dog.

'Woof-woof,' Gibblewort

answered hopefully.

But the dog wasn't fooled. He knew
dogs didn't smell like rotten fish.
They didn't look like them either.
He took a bite just to make sure.

'Yaroo!' howled Gibblewort,
and jumped clear.

He landed on a traffic island.
In the middle stood a tall pole,
with coloured lights. They kept
changing from green to amber to
red, then back to green again.

Now, goblins love coloured lights.
These had a button underneath,
a bit like the button in the bus.
Gibblewort pressed it to see what
would happen. The lights changed
more quickly. So he kept on
pressing it.

He was so dazzled by the lights
that he didn't notice the traffic
banking up. Or the red faces of
the drivers. Or all the hooting and
shouting.

'What's this then?' The policeman
was staring down at him again.
'You'd better come with me, sir.
You've become a public nuisance.'

CHAPTER
SIX

Gibblewort made a run for it.

The Policeman wasn't far behind.
Nor was the security guard from
the supermarket. And the kids from
the park. And the drivers from the
traffic jam. They chased him into
a cinema.

The film had just started. It was about dinosaurs.

Gibblewort's bulgy eyes nearly popped out.

'Is it the land of giants I'm in?' he said in a trembly voice. 'First it's houses big as mountains. Now it's lizards bigger than cows.'

The dinosaurs roared and showed their teeth. Gibblewort went so pale he shone in the dark.

'There he is!' voices cried.

Gibblewort ducked through the
nearest door. The policeman, the
security guard, the kids and the
drivers followed.

Down the hill sped Gibblewort,
dodging traffic all the way. At the
bottom, he came to the harbour.
The sight of so much water made
him shiver in his dirty skin.

'Not another giant bathtub!'
he groaned.

A ferry was about to leave.

'Come back, Mr Alien,' yelled
the kids.

'Stop that … that … that what-
d'you-call-it,' yelled the policeman.

'We'll teach you to block traffic,'
yelled the drivers.

'Stop thief!' yelled the security
guard.

Gibblewort leapt onto the ferry just as it chugged out into the harbour.

He thought he was safe at last. He thought wrong!

CHAPTER
SEVEN

Gibblewort poked out his tongue
at the people on shore. He flapped
his ears at them. He waggled his
nose until nasties fell out.

'Here's one goblin you'll not be
catchin' today!' he cried.

But he had spoken too soon. When he turned around, there were lots more kids on board. Worse still, they were staring in his direction.

They had never seen anyone as ugly as Gibblewort before. Or as dirty. They thought he looked pretty good. Like a monster in the movies or on TV.

'Yay!' cried the kids. 'Check out the movie star!'

They all wanted his autograph. Gibblewort didn't know this, of course. He just saw another bunch of kids rushing towards him. Some even had yukky ice creams and lollies in their hands!

'Yikes!' he screamed, and *jumped* overboard.

Straight into the giant bathtub!

'Oh, dearie-glub me-glub,' he moaned as he sank head-first.

'Clunk,' went his head on a rusty anchor.

'Clink-clunk,' went his feet as he trampled through the tin cans on the bottom.

When he waded ashore, he had
weed hanging from his ears. He had
rusted cans jammed on his feet.
He had bits of jellyfish stuck up his
nose. He had tiny fish swimming
behind his eyes.

'What is it?' people
asked in scared
voices.

'It must be a
sea serpent!'
others cried.

Most of them ran away. One brave
woman popped a plastic bag over
Gibblewort and tied it closed.

'The *museum* is the place for *you,*'
she said.

CHAPTER EIGHT

The people in the museum weren't sure about Gibblewort. Was he a fish? A lizard? Some kind of wormy creature with legs and arms?

They put him in a glass jar and poked at his belly with pointy things.

'Ouch!' said Gibblewort.

They squeezed his nose with tweezers.

'Ooh!' said Gibblewort.

They plucked hairs from his ears.

'Oi!' said Gibblewort.

They stared at him through
a magnifying glass.

'Eek!' he said, when he saw
how big their eyes looked.

'It's no good,' they said.
'He's something new. Let's
stuff him for display.'

'Stuff me!' Gibblewort screeched. 'I'll stuff you if I ever get out of here. Can't you see I'm a goblin?'

'A goblin?' They examined him more closely.

'Yes, an Irish goblin, and I want to go home.'

That was when Gibblewort started to cry. Green tears ran down his cheeks and splashed on the bottom of the jar. Soon the jar began to fill up.

'Can't someone-glub send me home-glub?' he pleaded.

The museum people didn't like
having their bottles filled with
smelly green tears. So they took
pity on him. They agreed to send
him back to Ireland.

'Aah, you're a lovely lot of fellers,'
Gibblewort said with relief. 'I'll
remember you in my goblin prayers.'

There his Australian adventures would have ended... except for one thing. The mailroom at the museum was full of stuff to be posted that day. So the person who sent him off had plenty of postbags to address. To lots of different places. And somehow (don't ask me how!) the postbags got mixed up.

I wonder which bag poor

Gibblewort was put into?

The Author

Victor Kelleher

Victor Kelleher was born in England and came to
Australia via Africa and New Zealand. After an
academic career he now writes both children's and
adult's novels full time from his home in Bellingen.
He has won and been shortlisted for many awards,
including the Children's Book Council of Australia Book
of the Year Award. His books with Random House
Australia include *Del-Del*, *To the Dark Tower*, *Beyond the
Dusk*, *Goblin in the Bush* and *Goblin on the Reef*.

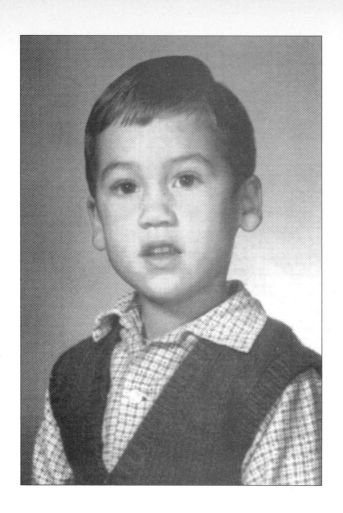

The Illustrator

Stephen Michael King

Stephen Michael King left school to pursue a career in nothing much. Trying to emulate Vincent Van Gogh, he twice dropped out of art school, eventually finding a job that suited him as a children's library assistant. After three years hanging out in the mind of a child, he moved into the serious world of the Walt Disney Sydney studios, before having his first book published – a 'how to draw cartoon animals' book. His first picture book, *The Man Who Loved Boxes,* was nominated for the Crighton Award for illustration, was the winner of the inaugural Family Award and was selected for Pick of the List (US). He has been shortlisted five times for a Children's Book Council Book of the Year Award and won both the 2002 YABBA and KOALA children's choice awards for *Pocket Dogs. Goblin in the Bush* was his first book with Random House Australia.